Mighty Mac

Based on *The Railway Series* by the Rev. W. Awdry

Illustrations by
Robin Davies and Phil Jacobs

EGMONT

EGMONT

We bring stories to life

First published in Great Britain in 2006
by Egmont UK Limited
239 Kensington High Street, London W8 6SA

Thomas the Tank Engine & Friends™

A BRITT ALLCROFT COMPANY PRODUCTION

Based on The Railway Series by The Reverend W Awdry
© 2007 Gullane (Thomas) LLC. A HIT Entertainment Company

Thomas the Tank Engine & Friends and Thomas & Friends are trademarks of Gullane (Thomas) Limited.
Thomas the Tank Engine & Friends and Design is Reg. US. Pat. & Tm. Off.

HiT entertainment

ISBN 978 1 4052 2654 7
3 5 7 9 10 8 6 4
Printed in Great Britain

The Forest Stewardship Council (FSC) is an international, non-governmental organisation
dedicated to promoting responsible management of the world's forests. FSC operates a
system of forest certification and product labelling that allows consumers to identify
wood and wood-based products from well managed forests.

For more information about Egmont's paper buying policy please visit www.egmont.co.uk/ethicalpublishing

For more information about the FSC please visit their website at www.fsc.uk.org

TO THE TRAINS ➡

This is a story about Mighty Mac, an engine with two faces! Mighty and Mac argued all the time. But one day they realised that if they didn't listen to each other, they could get into serious trouble . . .

The Island of Sodor is a very busy place in the summertime. Holiday-makers come from far and wide to sunbathe on the beaches and go for long walks in the beautiful hills.

Thomas and his Friends are kept very busy taking the holiday-makers from the Docks to their campsites.

"Toot, toot," whistle the engines as they race along the many tracks that cross the Island.

The engines were so busy The Fat Controller asked a new engine to come to the Island and help with the holiday rush.

The new engine's job would be to take holiday-makers to the mountain campsite. He had to be a very strong engine because the mountain track was very steep with lots of twists and turns.

Thomas was waiting at the Transfer Yards to welcome the new engine. He whistled a big, "Hello!"

"Hello!" came the reply from the engine.

It was followed very quickly by another, "Hello!"

Thomas looked from one end of the engine to the other. It had two faces! Thomas had never seen another engine like it.

"I'm Mighty," puffed the boiler with a curl on his head. "And I'm Mac," puffed the boiler with freckles. "Together we are Mighty Mac," they both puffed at once.

"Mighty Mac," called Mr Percival, The Thin Controller. "You are to take those holiday-makers to their mountain campsite."

"But how will we get to the holiday-makers?" groaned Mighty. "They are on the other side of the Yard."

"There were never so many tracks in the Shunting Yard we used to work in!" moaned Mac.

Luckily, Thomas was there to help them. "It's simple," he whistled. "Look where you want to go then follow the track that will take you there."

Mighty Mac looked at the tracks. Mighty began to chuff carefully in one direction.

Mac had other ideas. "You are going the wrong way!" he puffed, trying to pull back along a different track.

"No, it's this way!" chugged Mighty, pushing Mac along another track.

Very soon they were going backwards and forwards along the tracks, they even had a ride on the turntable, but they didn't seem to be getting any closer to the holiday-makers.

"We're here!" Mighty suddenly whistled. "Oh, really," chuffed Mac. "Then why are the passengers over there?"

Mighty Mac looked across the tracks at the holiday-makers still waiting on the platform. Mighty Mac certainly wasn't a Really Useful Engine.

"Now you are late!" said Mr Percival, angrily.

"Follow me," puffed Thomas. He showed Mighty Mac how to cross over to the holiday-makers.

"We'll have to work extra hard," chuffed Mighty Mac. "We have to get to the campsite before it gets dark."

Mighty Mac chugged quickly up the mountain track. "This way," puffed Mighty, when they came to a fork in the track. He began to follow the left track.

"No, this way!" called Mac. But Mighty didn't listen. "It's this way," puffed Mac crossly and he pulled and pushed Mighty along another track.

"Be careful!" cried the holiday-makers, who were being bumped and bounced inside the carriage.

Suddenly, Mighty Mac came to a dead end. Mighty and Mac had been too busy arguing to pay attention to where the campsite was. Some rocks had fallen on the track and Mighty Mac couldn't go any further.

"This isn't our campsite," said the holiday-makers.

"This is your fault," puffed Mac, giving Mighty a shove. "No, it's yours!" chugged Mighty, shoving him back.

Little by little Mighty Mac's shoving and pushing began to nudge the carriage, until they were bumping so quickly they knocked the carriage off the rails.

"We'll never get to the campsite now," grumbled the holiday-makers.

"This is your fault," Mighty told Mac. "No, it's your fault!" Mac was sure.

"1, 2, 3, Push!" the holiday-makers were working together to get the carriage back on the tracks. Mighty Mac watched them helping each other.

"Ok, you lead, this time, Mac," said Mighty. "Let's go down the track so the passengers can couple me to the carriage."

"Good idea – let's work together!" puffed Mac.

"Well done!" cheered the holiday-makers.

When Mighty and Mac worked together they found they could do anything.

Mighty could see the flag flying high above the campsite at the bottom of the mountain. "Let's go!" he whistled.

"Hold on!" said Mac. "Which way is it to the campsite?"

"Remember what Thomas told us," puffed Mighty, brightly.

"Look where you want to go," puffed Mac.

"Then follow the track that will take you there," chuffed Mighty.

"You know, Mac," wheeshed Mighty, "when we pull together and work together . . ."

". . . we can be a Really Useful Engine!" whistled Mac. And they set off happily back down the mountain.

The Thomas Story Library is THE definitive collection of stories about Thomas and ALL his Friends.

5 more Thomas Story Library titles will be chuffing into your local bookshop in April 2007:

Arthur

Caroline

Murdoch

Neville

Freddie

And there are even more
Thomas Story Library books to follow later!
So go on, start your Thomas Story Library NOW!

A Fantastic Offer for Thomas the Tank Engine Fans!

STICK POUND COIN HERE

In every Thomas Story Library book like this one, you will find a special token. Collect 6 Thomas tokens and we will send you a brilliant Thomas poster, and a double-sided bedroom door hanger! Simply tape a £1 coin in the space above, and fill out the form overleaf.

TO BE COMPLETED BY AN ADULT

To apply for this great offer, ask an adult to complete the coupon below
and send it with a pound coin and 6 tokens, to:
THOMAS OFFERS, PO BOX 715, HORSHAM RH12 5WG

☐ Please send a Thomas poster and door hanger. I enclose 6 tokens
plus a £1 coin. (Price includes P&P)

Fan's name..

Address..

....Postcode....................................

Date of birth..

Name of parent/guardian...

Signature of parent/guardian...

Please allow 28 days for delivery. Offer is only available while stocks last. We reserve the right to change
the terms of this offer at any time and we offer a 14 day money back guarantee. This does not affect your
statutory rights.

☐ Data Protection Act: If you do not wish to receive other similar offers from us or companies we
recommend, please tick this box. Offers apply to UK only.

Cut along the dotted line